The Magic at Villa Verde

Maryam Nemazie

Illustrations by Gale Kenison

Balboa Press books may be ordered through booksellers or by contacting:

Balboa Press
A Division of Hay House
1663 Liberty Drive
Bloomington, IN 47403
www.balboapress.com
1 (877) 407-4847

Because of the dynamic nature of the Internet, any web addresses or links contained in this book may have changed since publication and may no longer be valid. The views expressed in this work are solely those of the author and do not necessarily reflect the views of the publisher, and the publisher hereby disclaims any responsibility for them.

Any people depicted in stock imagery provided by Getty Images are models, and such images are being used for illustrative purposes only.
Certain stock imagery © Getty Images.

Interior Image Credit: Gale Kenison

ISBN: 978-1-9822-4617-4 (sc)
ISBN: 978-1-9822-4616-7 (e)

Library of Congress Control Number: 2020906944

Print information available on the last page.

Balboa Press rev. date: 05/01/2020

BALBOA.PRESS
A DIVISION OF HAY HOUSE

Dedication

First and foremost, I dedicate this book in honor of my grandmother, Esmat ("Essie") Ghaffari, who was my inspiration and muse. I always wanted to write a book, but it wasn't until after her passing that the first character, Essie the Elephant, was born in my imagination.

I also dedicate this book to my parents for their eternal love and support; my husband, who is my soul mate; and my daughter, who is my heart.

Last, but certainly not least, I dedicate this book to Gale Kenison. With her artwork, Gale precisely captured the feelings of each character through my eyes. You are forever in my heart.

Thank you to my family and friends for bringing the magic of Villa Verde alive.

Contents

Acknowledgments

I would like to take this opportunity to thank Balboa Press and Louise Hay for creating a mechanism for aspiring authors like me to take the leap and self-publish their work. I would love to acknowledge Gale Kenison for her imagination and creativity in bringing to life the characters of Villa Verde. Without her dedication, this dream of mine would not be possible. Lastly, I would like to acknowledge all the wise thinkers who have been writing, singing, and teaching about self-discovery for ages. It is my hope to bring these lifelong principles to youth at an earlier age. Now more than ever, our planet needs young leaders awake and ready to light the way with love.

01 Essie the Elephant — Love Yourself

Essie the Elephant was the most magnificent of all the creatures.
She was majestic, grand, and had beautiful features.

Unfortunately, Essie had gigantic issues.
She was always crying and wiping away tears with tissues.

As she was so testy, Essie had only one friend, Homa the Hen.
Homa was wise and gentle, and her sword was the pen.

Essie and Homa lived in Villa Verde, a beautiful place in the hills.
It was home to many animals and filled with many thrills.

One day Essie was complaining to Homa that being an elephant was ridiculous.
Homa was in awe; she had never heard anything so ludicrous.

Essie looked at Homa with a pouty face.
"Look at my long nose. It's such a disgrace!"

Homa the Hen shook her head in disbelief.
She muttered to Essie, "Oh, good grief!"

"In fact, Essie, I think your long nose is super cool.
You can use it to wipe your drool!"

"That's my point, Homa—I don't like my nose."
Homa responded, "I'm sure you can find a use for it. How about as a hose?"

Essie had never heard of anything so silly and stomped away, super mad.
Homa was just trying to help, but obviously she didn't, and felt very bad.

One summer day, Kathy and Sam, the owners of Villa Verde, had a very special guest.
Their granddaughter, Kayla, was visiting for the day, dressed in her Sunday best.

Kathy told Kayla to have fun in the sun.
Kayla was an adventurous girl who loved to climb and run.

Kayla roamed about Villa Verde and was fascinated by the tall magnolia tree.
Kayla decided that she wanted to climb it, even though she kept bumping her knee.

Homa saw Kayla quickly climbing the magnolia tree higher and higher.
Homa thought that this situation could become quite dire.

Sure enough, Kayla climbed too high and was scared to come down.
Her beautiful smile was replaced by a worried frown.

"Grandma! Grandpa!" shouted Kayla. "Come find me."
Homa had an idea and found Essie as quick as could be.

"Essie! Essie! Come quickly. Kayla is stuck up the magnolia tree. What can we do?"
Essie followed Homa to the tree. Her thoughts were jumbled like a vegetable stew.

"Homa, let's see how high my long nose can go."
Homa nodded in agreement, nervously pacing to and fro.

Essie's long nose inched up higher and higher.
In fact, Essie's nose was extremely powerful and could even put out a fire.

Essie's trunk reached to where Kayla was sitting.
And Essie wrapped her nose around Kayla, which was very fitting.

Essie then gently lowered her trunk until Kayla was safely back on the ground.
Kayla was happy and started laughing, which to Essie's ears was the most beautiful sound.

Kayla then gave Essie a big hug and kiss.
Essie was in a state of pure bliss.

Kayla whispered in Essie's big, floppy ear,
"I love you and your beautiful nose. Thanks to you, I have nothing to fear."

Essie looked bashfully at Homa and started to blush.
"You were right, Homa. Next time I say something negative about my nose, please tell me to hush!"

Homa responded, "Don't you worry; I will remind you to cherish what makes you unique."
"Yes, Homa. I'll think twice before I speak.

"Spoken words come from thoughts, and your thoughts become your reality.
From now on, I will love everything about me."

8

02 Baichan the Bunny — It Takes a Team

Kayla's best friend was Baichan the Bunny.
Their relationship was as sweet as honey.

Kayla and Baichan loved to play all day long.
"Twinkle, Twinkle, Little Star" was their favorite song.

Baichan had the biggest heart. It was made of pure gold.
She knew how to make anyone smile, even those who were very cold.

As a bunny, Baichan could run extremely fast.
In a race, she was never last.

One day, Kayla and Baichan decided to play hide-and-go-seek.
Baichan said, "I'll go hide first. Promise not to peek!"

Kayla shut her eyes and counted quickly to ten.
When she opened her eyes, she saw Homa the Hen.

"Homa, did you see which way Baichan went?"
"No, sorry, Kayla. Maybe you should look in your tent."

Kayla decided to try Homa's suggestion and skipped away.
But Baichan was nowhere to be found, and Kayla had been searching all day.

"Baichan, Baichan, where are you? Come out, come out, wherever you are."
When Baichan didn't come out, Kayla decided to drive around in her little car.

Kayla drove to Essie the Elephant and asked if she had seen her bunny.
Essie shook her head no. "Maybe it's time to stop looking. It's no longer sunny."

Essie was right. There was very little light.
But Kayla felt that something wasn't quite right.

12

Kayla knew she had to think outside the box.
She drove her car to go see Ferdosi the Fox.

Ferdosi the Fox was the cleverest animal that Kayla had ever met.
Ferdosi could solve any problem and never lost a bet.

"Ferdosi, Ferdosi! I need your help! Baichan is nowhere to be found."
"Don't worry. I'll send out Heydari the Hound."

Heydari the Hound sniffed all around.
And still, Baichan was nowhere to be found.

Ferdosi put his thinking cap on and listened to all the sounds.
He called Gary the Gopher to search the entire grounds.

Gary was special because he could look for Baichan under the dirt.
But when Gary reported that Baichan was still missing, Kayla looked so hurt.

Ferdosi was frustrated and looked up at the sky with great disdain.
Then he saw Eraj the Eagle soaring through the clouds like an airplane.

"That's it! I have the best idea. I know it will do the trick."
Ferdosi called out, "Eraj, Eraj! Come here; please be quick!"

"Baichan is missing. She may be in danger."
Kayla added, "I hope she wasn't taken by a stranger."

Eraj said, "Don't you worry, Kayla. I will find her no matter what it takes."
Kayla climbed on Eraj's back, and they flew up high in the sky over the lakes.

Eraj asked the fish to search the waters, but Baichan was not there.
Kayla was worried and shouted, "This is not fair!"

Just then, Eraj heard a yelp.
It was Baichan, yelling for help.

Eraj then saw an old water well.
It turned out that Baichan was inside, where she fell.

Eraj flew and pulled Baichan out of the water.
Baichan was in shock and started to stutter.

"I thought no one would ever be able to find me in that deep, dark well."
Kayla replied, "We were all looking for you for hours." Tears started to well.

Eraj flew back to Ferdosi and all the other animals, who were still trying to come up
with more rescue plans to save the day.
Kayla shouted, "Eraj found Baichan. Hip, hip hooray!"

Eraj humbly said, "We found Baichan because we all worked together as a team."
Ferdosi answered, "Thanks to each other, we didn't run out of steam."
Eraj wisely replied, "If everyone could learn how to work together, then life would be like a dream."

Baichan said, "Thanks to all of you who didn't give up looking for me.
I am so blessed to have you all as my friends. You are my collaborative community."

Eraj the Eagle ended the day with a special message.
"Friends, we should always think good thoughts, speak kindly, and do good deeds.
If we just live by these principles, we can accomplish any task and fulfill all our needs."

The animals of Villa Verde went to sleep that night with hearts full and minds at ease because they knew they could count on each other and live together happily in peace.

03 Laila the Ladybug — Unleash Your Power, and Shine like a Star

Laila the Ladybug was Villa Verde's unique creature.
Ladybugs were red with black dots, but Laila had a special feature.

Her dots were a sparkling gold that glittered in the sun.
While Laila's colors were exquisite, other ladybugs liked to poke fun.

Laila desperately wanted to fit in.
But no matter what she did, Laila was in a battle she just couldn't win.

Laila was a fantastic artist. She even tried to paint her dots black like all the other ladybugs. Unfortunately, it didn't work. Laila didn't receive any acknowledgments, smiles, or hugs.

After many attempts, Laila decided she would be fine on her own.
She spent her days reading, painting, and wearing gowns she had sown.

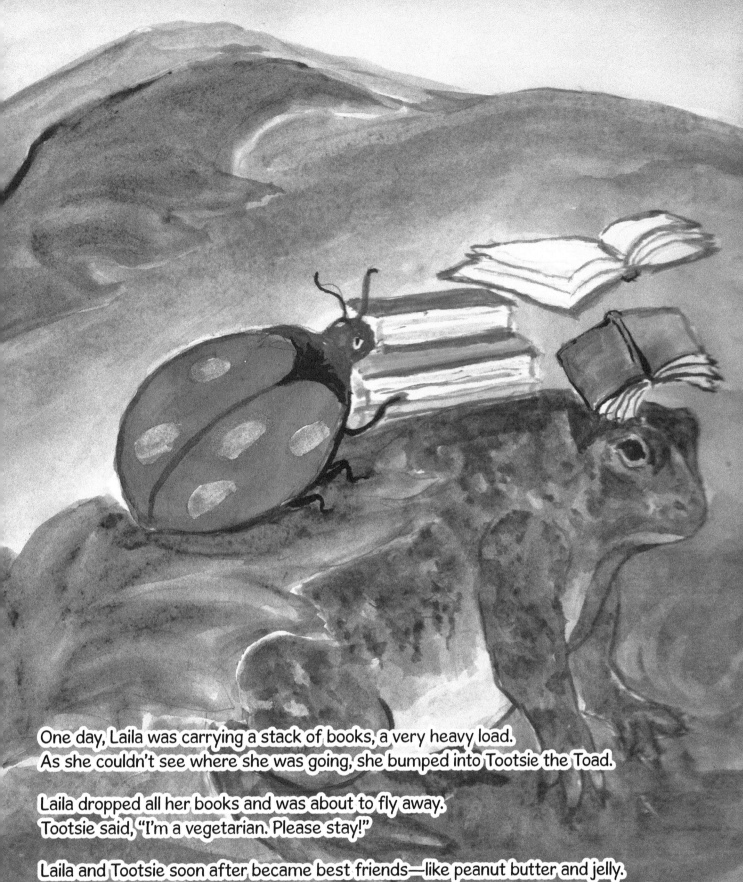

One day, Laila was carrying a stack of books, a very heavy load.
As she couldn't see where she was going, she bumped into Tootsie the Toad.

Laila dropped all her books and was about to fly away.
Tootsie said, "I'm a vegetarian. Please stay!"

Laila and Tootsie soon after became best friends—like peanut butter and jelly.
Like Laila, Tootsie didn't have any friends because she looked funny and was smelly.

Laila didn't care about such superficial things.
She was able to see the true essence of all beings.

One day, Laila and Tootsie were relaxing in the sun.
From a distance, they saw Sheila the Spider on the run.

Sheila was being chased by dragonflies, who were looking for their next meal.
Laila and Tootsie came up with a plan as the dragonflies were right on Sheila's heel.

Laila flew in the sky, and her golden, glittery dots caught the sun's rays,
creating a bright light that could make someone blind for days.

Laila flashed the light toward the dragonflies so they couldn't see.
Then one by one, Tootsie used his tongue to put them in captivity.
Sheila exclaimed, "You saved my life. Thank you for my serenity."

Sheila was so happy to become friends with Laila and Tootsie because she was a lonely outsider.
Most creatures feared her, and when they saw her shouted, "Eeek! A spider!"

Laila, Tootsie, and Sheila spent their time together having fun.
But then the very next day, they heard the sound of the dragonflies' wings going *hummmm.*

They were ready, and Sheila began to weave her web as fast as she could.
The dragonflies were heading to where all the ladybugs rested on a long piece of wood.

Laila flew before all the ladybugs and glistened in the sun, so brilliant and bright, blinding all the dragonflies, allowing Tootsie to flick them all in Sheila's web; they couldn't even put up a fight!

Laila then flew toward the web and said, "We are willing to let you all go, even the dragonflies we caught yesterday, on one condition:
Promise to leave the insects of Villa Verde alone. Otherwise, we will capture all of you. It will be our mission!"

The dragonflies agreed to Laila's terms and even signed a peace treaty promising never to do any harm.
All the ladybugs swarmed around Laila, singing her praise and admiring her charm.

Laila's glittery, golden dots were finally accepted by the ladybugs.
Laila now received nothing but acknowledgments, smiles, and hugs.

Laila wisely said, "There was a time when I desperately wanted to fit in and just be ordinary.
But then I realized that this would not be possible because I am extraordinary.
I have found friends who love and accept me.
I discovered that I can't live my life for the approval of others, and I am finally free.
I will once again fly with the ladybugs with great pride.
I will make sure that you all embrace every being. Those who are different will have no need to hide.
For our differences are what make us who we are.
We just have to unleash this power, and shine like a star!"

Jasper the Giraffe was the only giraffe at Villa Verde.
He loved his tall neck because he was able to spend time in trees all day.

Jasper would chat with the birds high up in the trees.
He was so friendly that he even spent time with bumblebees.

Jasper's long neck gave him the advantage to see far off into the distance.
Jasper knew how to go with the flow and always chose the path of least resistance.

Jasper's passion was playing sports.
Jasper also loved to build forts.

One day, the animals of Villa Verde were scheduling tryouts for a soccer team.
This was Jasper's opportunity to pursue his dream.

Jasper knew he had what it took to make the cut.
However, with Jasper, there was one big *but*.

Jasper was worried something would go wrong.
He decided to practice every day and just stay mentally strong.

Jasper only had one week to get ready for the tryouts.
He was ready to work hard and put away his doubts.

However, the weather was getting hot and icky.
Jasper was sweaty and sticky.

Meena the Mosquito was buzzing around the leaves.
She landed on one of Jasper's knees.

Meena put her stinger deep inside.
"Ouch, that hurts!" Jasper cried.

But Meena the Mosquito wouldn't stop her stinging.
Jasper would scratch and scratch until his skin started bleeding.

Flying up in the sky, Karen the Crane saw Jasper in pain.
She swooped down and gobbled up Meena with great disdain.

Karen said, "I can't believe that mosquito was attacking you."
Jasper responded, "I was training for the tryouts, but I'm a mess now. What am I going to do?"

Karen said firmly, "You don't allow others to throw you off from your chosen path."
Jasper returned to his training after a nice warm bath.

Jasper practiced every minute until the big day.
When he made the team, Karen shouted a big
"Hurray!"

So if you ever see a beautiful white crane, it's
a reminder to stay strong.
And no matter what, you should always sing
your song!

05

Sahar the Squirrel — There Isn't Anything that Love Can't Mend

Sahar the Squirrel is the friendliest squirrel you will ever meet.
Spending time with her is such a joyous treat.

A sage is very wise and gives good advice.
And Sahar shared her wisdom without any price.

Sahar would help any being that was in need.
She also made sure to do a good deed.

All the squirrels loved Sahar except one.
His name was Sammy, and he was no fun.

Sammy was competitive and wanted to be the best.
He was working so hard, like he had to ace a test.

But Sahar never let Sammy get under her skin
for she knew how to go deep within.

You see, Sahar knew the secret powers of finding her inner peace.
All the animals visited Sahar to learn her secrets, even Sammy's niece.

One day, Sammy was on the run.
He was trying to outshine the sun.

Sahar the Squirrel watched Sammy from high in the trees.
She saw Sammy collecting nuts, getting ready for the winter freeze.

Sammy was hiding his food in a secret burrow.
But Sammy wasn't very thorough.

The birds had found Sammy's secret stash.
They were stealing his food and having a bash.

Sahar went to tell Sammy what was going on with his food.
But Sammy ignored her and was in a very mean mood.

Sahar stayed far away.
But she would always pray.

She prayed that Sammy would come around.
For with him, kindness was nowhere to be found.

The winter freeze came along.
All the birds flew away without singing a song.

Sammy went to his hidden burrow to get a meal.
He saw his stash was gone and wondered, *Who would steal?*

Sammy started accusing all the squirrels one by one.
He became so cruel that no one would talk to him, not even a nun.

After time had passed, Sammy's tummy was starting to growl.
Sammy had no choice but to go on the prowl.

Sahar saw Sammy out in the cold.
Sammy was no longer so bold.

He asked everyone to give him some food.
But no one wanted to help him because he was so rude.

Sahar offered Sammy a hand.
She invited him to her sacred land.

At first, Sammy was too proud to admit defeat.
Sahar wisely said, "Come on, Sammy; I will give you a treat."

Sahar gave Sammy his favorite honey-covered nuts.
Sammy started crying. "I'm sorry, Sahar; I've been such a putz!"

Sahar said, "I forgive you, Sammy, for being so rude.
But now it's time to start being a nicer dude."

"How can I start over? Everyone hates me," said Sammy.
Tears were pouring down his face, and his paws were clammy.

Sahar said, "Don't worry. I'll help you.
But first, let's eat this yummy stew."

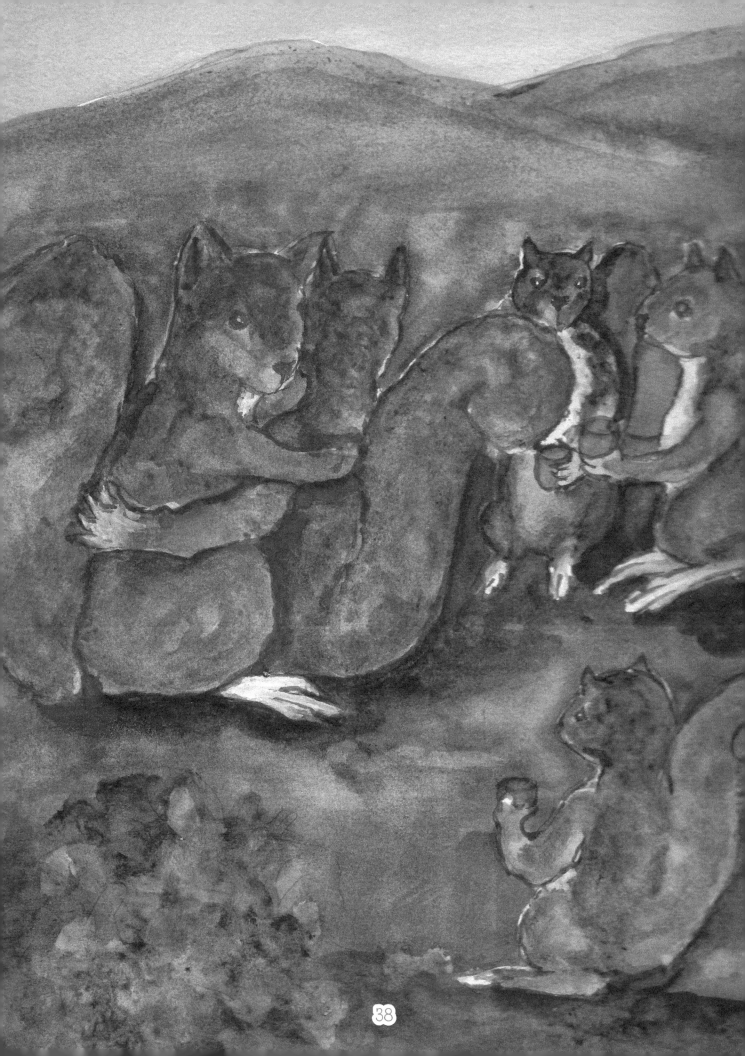

Sammy visited all the squirrels and said he was sorry for what he had done.
He promised he would be less crabby and start having fun.

Over time, Sahar became Sammy's best friend,
proving once again that there isn't anything love can't mend.

Many squirrels asked Sahar how she could forgive Sammy for being so cruel.
Sahar replied, "I knew not to take anything personally. It was Sammy who was being a fool."

But thankfully, Sammy saw the error of his ways.
Now he can enjoy life all the days.

06

Daddy the Dolphin — Teach Others How to Catch a Fish instead of Giving Them a Fish

At Villa Verde there was a fabulous pool.
It was home to Daddy the Dolphin, who liked to stay cool.

Daddy was a protector, taking care of the large and the small.
Daddy loved sports and could use his nose to balance a ball.

Daddy was extremely observant, seeing all there was to see.
And he knew how to go with the flow and simply be.

One sunny day little Kayla came outside to play.
She was eager to swim now that it was the month of May.

Unfortunately, she was not quite ready to swim on her own.
"Grandma, come swim with me." Kayla started to groan.

But Grandma couldn't hear Kayla's groans from far away.
Kayla was growing impatient and couldn't keep her frustration at bay.

All the while, Daddy was watching Kayla from under the deep blue,
waiting to see what she was going to do.

Sure enough, Kayla walked to the edge of the pool,
too young to know she was being a fool.

Kayla dipped a toe in, just to see how it would feel.
But she lost her balance, and up went her heel.

She fell into the deep end with no floaty or vest.
Daddy was ready in rescue mode; this was no time to rest.

He swam under Kayla and told her to hold on to him tight.
Daddy bolted to the surface with all of his might.

Jumping out of the water and gliding along,
Kayla was having so much fun and started singing a song.

Even though Daddy had saved the day,
he wanted Kayla to always be safe, even if she
came again in harm's way.

Daddy said, "Kayla, if you learn
how to swim, I'll give you a
treasure.
But if you don't want to, you
don't have to. There is no
pressure."

Kayla responded, "Teach me;
teach me. I want to swim like a
mermaid.
I know I can do it. I won't be
afraid."

42

Daddy swam with Kayla for hours and hours
until he had taught her all of his swimming powers.

Kayla mastered swimming with a different stroke.
Daddy was so proud of her. No joke!

He presented Kayla with a beautiful box made from a seashell.
Kayla was so touched that tears started to well.

Inside was a beautiful necklace with a pearl.
It was the perfect gift for a little girl.

Kayla hugged Daddy and gave him a kiss.
Kayla then whispered to Daddy, "I love you. You are my bliss."

07 Kathy the Queen Bee — The Power of Love

Kathy is the queen bee of Villa Verde.
She knows how to have a fantastic day.

For you see, Kathy has a personality warmer than the sun.
When you are with her, you will have nothing but fun.

Kathy is so loving and kind.
Everyone in her presence has peace of mind.

Except one evil little creature
who had a very nasty feature.

Her heart was as black as coal.
She isolated herself in a dark hole.

She was short and tiny.
And her hair was always grimy.

She didn't have a name; she was just a flea.
She had no heart as you will clearly see.

The flea was so jealous that Kathy was a queen.
She wanted to do something really mean.

She thought about it day after day,
just how to make Kathy's skies gray.

All the while, Kathy had no clue.
She was so sunny that nothing made her blue.

One day, the flea decided to jump on Kathy's heart and suck the blood away.
But no matter how much she tried, she was in dismay.

For believe it or not, Kathy had magical powers.
The flea sucked for hours and hours.

But in the end, the flea could not win.
Her wicked head started to spin.

She realized she was no match for Kathy the Queen
because Kathy's heart had a love no other had seen.

Her heart was so strong and pure.
There was nothing that it couldn't cure.

The flea finally admitted defeat.
She knew she could no longer compete.

She packed her bags and left Villa Verde.
All of the animals shouted, "Hooray!"

Kathy wisely said, "You have a power inside you that is tried and true.
All that you need to do is say, 'I love you.'

"For the power of love is like no other,
just like the love of a mother.

"If you ever feel that someone is not true,
look within yourself to know what to do.

"Let love pour out from your heart like the rays of the sun.
Hence, your work here on Planet Earth is done.

"For we are here to share our love.
Peace will come like a beautiful white dove.

"Next time you encounter an evil creature,
don't forget your magnificent feature.

"Let your power of love shine through.
Your heart will guide you in everything you do."

Mimi the Mermaid was the most beautiful creature in the sea.
She was kind, gentle, and as sweet as could be.

Mimi lived in the sea bordering Villa Verde.
She was a protector and guarded the property all day.

Mimi made sure that Villa Verde was safe and sound.
She was so watchful, even more than a basset hound.

Mimi's most precious treasure was a creamy white pearl.
Her father had given it to her when she was a little girl.

This pearl had magical powers.
Mimi would guard it for hours and hours.

Mimi would hold the pearl and make a wish.
It would come true as fast as a shark chasing a fish.

One day, Mimi was as busy as a bee.
She was focused and didn't see.

Ellie the Eel slithered by.
Ellie was so mean that she would make even babies cry.

Ellie's eyes were growing with greed.
You see, she was in a desperate need.

Her need was for the magic of the precious pearl
because she was such a miserable girl.

Ellie stole Mimi's pearl with no remorse.
She galloped away on her little seahorse.

When Mimi discovered her pearl was missing, she was crushed.
She started crying, and her face was flushed.

Mimi closed her eyes and wished to find her pearl.
Suddenly, the treasure appeared in Mimi's hand with a whirl.

Mimi couldn't believe it. She was the one that had magical powers all along.
Mimi looked at the pearl and asked aloud, "Who did me wrong?"

Suddenly, Ellie appeared before Mimi's eyes.
Immediately, she started sputtering lies.

Ellie said, "Oh, Mimi, it wasn't I who took your pearl.
You wouldn't think I am that type of girl?

"Anyway, this pearl isn't all that magical.
I made a wish, and it was so impractical!

"How could I think my wish would come true?
Now I am sad and very blue."

"Please tell me your wish," Mimi said with a smile.
"Don't give up yet, though it may be your style."

Ellie was shocked. "Why would you care to know after what I've done?
I don't deserve any kindness from you or anything fun!"

Mimi said wisely, "I will forgive you and let the past go.
You must have had a good reason to do something so low."

"Yes," said Ellie in a soft voice.
"You see, I had no choice.

"I wanted to use the magic of the pearl to find a friend.
I am so lonely, and there is no relationship that I can mend.

"Everyone knows me as Ellie the Evil Eel.
I'm tired of eating alone at every single meal."

Mimi gave Ellie a warm hug and said, "I can make your wish come true.
Now join me for some fresh Ghormeh Sabzee stew."

From that moment on, Ellie was no longer evil as sin
because Mimi taught Ellie how to treasure the power within.

While the art of forgiveness is very hard to do,
its power is tried and true.

Those who know how to forgive and let go are few and far between.
But just try it, and your life will become so serene.

Salma the Swan was Villa Verde's most elegant creature.
Not only was she beautiful: she was smart, like a teacher.

Salma was very wise.
She was always healthy, except when eating her favorite french fries.

Salma was glamorous, fancy, and trendy.
Her favorite purse was a vintage Fendi.

Salma lived on a beautiful pond surrounded by willow trees.
She knew the ways of the birds and the bees.

Salma's feathers were as white as snow.
She knew how to sit back and enjoy the show.

Salma was always there for a friend in need.
Always doing a good deed.

Even if it meant putting herself in harm's way
for there was nothing she wouldn't do to save the day.

Of all the swans, Salma's feathers were unique.
She was the one with the best physique.

The other swans were green with envy.
Their jealousy put them in a state of frenzy.

The other swans came up with a wicked plan.
While Salma was asleep, they poured black tar on her and ran.

The next day, Salma was as black as night.
But she didn't mind and embraced her fate with all her might.

Casey the Caretaker smelled the tar from faraway.
He approached Salma and asked her if she was okay.

Salma calmly said, "Yes, I am fine. Why do you ask?"
Casey replied in shock, "You are covered in tar! I'll clean it off. It will be my task."

Casey was the caretaker of all the animals at Villa Verde.
He was kind to all the animals in his special way.

Casey was so patient and caring to creatures great and small.
He was always in nature. You would never find him at the mall.

Casey spent hours cleaning the tar off each and every feather.
There was no storm that Casey couldn't weather.

The toxic tar was finally gone.
It took so long it was nearly dawn.

Salma thanked Casey with all of her heart.
She was so grateful that he was so smart.

For the tar would have made her very sick,
just like a bite from a tiny tick.

Now that Salma was again as healthy as could be,
she spread her wings, and from the tar she was free.

Life may have its twists and turns.
Sometimes it may make your heart burn.

The universe will bring you what you need.
Just have faith and plant that seed.

10 Mommy the Meerkat — The Awakening

There once was a mommy who just had a baby.
She was sweet, kind, and definitely a lady.

Mommy was insecure about taking care of a little child,
for when the baby was fussy, Mommy would go wild.

At Villa Verde, Mommy was busy moving to and fro.
She did not know how to stop and go with the flow.

Mommy was tired of going all around.
She wanted to get lost and never be found.

So, Mommy planned to leave Villa Verde for a fun trip.
She wanted to take Daddy on a cruise ship.

Daddy's birthday was in the month of May,
and Mommy planned to travel to an island far away.

Mommy was excited for what the trip would bring.
She was at peace; she could hear the angels sing.

When they got to the island, Mommy was ready to have some fun.
But Daddy wanted to relax on the beach, under the sun.

Mommy went and talked to a guide.
She heard there was a magical garden within a five-minute ride.

Mommy wanted to see the magical garden while they were here.
Daddy said, "Sure, let's go and see the garden, my dear."

Mommy and Daddy started off on their quest.
But along the way, they ran into a pest.

magical Garden →

GUIDE

Mommy got bitten from head to toe.
She was itchy and crabby; oh no!

Mommy did not know what to say.
She felt like her skies were gray.

Daddy said, "We will see the magical garden soon."
But the very next day, they were stuck in a monsoon!

A few days went by, and Mommy was going crazy.
She wanted to see the garden even though the sky was hazy.

Mommy heard the garden held the key to inner bliss.
She needed that, so it was a place she didn't want to miss.

Mommy thought, *I will see this garden, rain or shine!*
If I have to go by myself, that is totally fine.

Mommy walked for hours and hours with no end in sight.
The sun was starting to go down, and soon there would be no light.

Sweaty and hungry, it was no paradise.
Mommy was still itchy all over, like she was covered with lice.

Mommy heard a sound from behind the trees.
She thought it sounded like a swarm of bees.

But it turned out to be a puppy that had also lost its way.
Mommy was thinking, *What a crazy day!*

Mommy looked on the collar and read the name "Coco."
She also saw an address, and they were on the go.

After walking for a while, Mommy found the home.
Mommy and Coco no longer had to roam.

Sophia the Sand Cat was looking for Coco all around.
She never thought Coco would be found.

Sophia said, "You are so kind.
I almost lost my mind."

Mommy said, "I found Coco while searching for a magical garden in haste."
Sophia responded, "Oh, sweetie, your search has not gone to waste.

"You see, you've been in the magical garden all along.
But you had so many thoughts in your head that you did not know right from wrong."

In that moment, Mommy woke from her state of slumber.
She realized that she needed to get Sophia's number.

For Sophia's wise words went straight to her heart.
And when Mommy returned to Ville Verde, her life had a new start.

Mommy realized that the problem was in her head all along.
She needed to go within to find her own special song.

For it doesn't matter where you are.
If you are not awake, you won't get very far.

Wake up from your deep, deep sleep.
Go ahead, and take that leap.

Enlightenment is within your reach.
Once you get there, every day will be like a walk on the beach.

No matter what comes your way,
you won't let it spoil your day.

Inner bliss cannot be bought or sold.
You will need to break the mold.

So do the work, and find your special song,
for it is within you all along!

CPSIA information can be obtained
at www.ICGtesting.com
Printed in the USA
BVHW020953220720
584317BV00003B/42